ziggy and the Black Dinosaurs

The Buried Bones Mystery

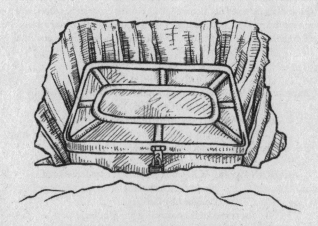

By Sharon M. Draper
Illustrated by Jesse Joshua Watson

Aladdin Paperbacks
New York London Toronto Sydney

For Wendy, Damon, Cory, and Crystal

❧

ALADDIN PAPERBACKS
An imprint of Simon & Schuster Children's Publishing Division
1230 Avenue of the Americas, New York, NY 10020
Text copyright © 1994, 2006 by Sharon M. Draper
Illustrations copyright © 2006 by Simon & Schuster, Inc.
All rights reserved, including the right of reproduction
in whole or in part in any form.
ALADDIN PAPERBACKS and colophon are trademarks of
Simon & Schuster, Inc.
Designed by Lisa Vega
The text of this book was set in Minion.
Manufactured in the United States of America
First Aladdin Paperbacks edition January 2006
This book, in slightly different format,
was originally published by Just Us Books.
2   4   6   8   10   9   7   5   3
Library of Congress Control Number 2005924765
ISBN-13: 978-0-689-87910-4
ISBN-10: 0-689-87910-5

One

School was over and the summer morning stretched ahead like a soft, sweet piece of bubble gum. It was still early for a boy who had just finished fifth grade and promised himself he would sleep until noon every day of summer vacation. But the day was warm, and no matter how he tried to ignore it, the sunshine had called him early to get up. Rico Johnson grabbed his basketball and headed down the street to Ziggy's house.

Rico liked to go to Ziggy's house because it was so different from his own. Rico lived with his mom, who drove a dull brown car and worked in an office building downtown, where she wore sensible, flat shoes and wrote careful letters to people in other offices. She went bowling with her friends every Friday night and took Rico to piano lessons every Saturday afternoon. She was the kind of mom who didn't think dinner was complete unless a green vegetable was served. *Basically boring,* thought Rico.

But Ziggy's house—now that was another story. It was huge, brightly painted, and cheerful. Ziggy's mom sometimes planted flowers and sometimes vegetables in the front yard, so there was an odd assortment of tomato plants, roses, corn, and lilies growing together. The grass was cut whenever someone thought about it. One summer it had even been kept short by Ziggy's uncle Raphael's pet goat. Trimmed or not, it always looked soft and inviting, and was the perfect place to stop and rest on a hot day.

Ziggy's doorbell didn't work, so Rico knocked on the screen door. Raphael came to the door looking sleepy and confused. His hair, long and braided, hung down over his eyes.

"So, little mon, you come see Ziggy?" Rico grinned and nodded. "Him still sleep—go get his lazy bones up, mon."

Raphael let Rico in and headed back to bed to finish his morning nap. Three more uncles and a cousin were staying with Ziggy's family, but the house still felt large and roomy. Ziggy's mom came from a family of fourteen in Jamaica, so she kept her door open to any relative who needed a place to stay.

Rico had spent the night at Ziggy's many times, so he knew exactly where he was headed. He ran up the stairs, turned left, and opened the bathroom door. There, in the bathtub, wrapped in an army sleeping bag, lay Ziggy. He was wide awake.

"I been waiting for you, mon," said Ziggy with a grin. "What's up?"

"Not you, man. Why you still sleepin' in the tub? You got a perfectly good bed right across the hall."

"Ah, Rico-mon, a soft bed is for sissies! I'm practicing for when I become a spy for the FB of I. Spies gotta be tough, you know. Besides, when I gotta get up and go to the bathroom at night, I'm already there!"

Rico laughed and helped Ziggy out of the tub. Ziggy got dressed, brushed his teeth, grabbed his basketball, put on a large black, yellow, and green hat his mother had knitted, and tucked his braids inside. Then he and Rico headed downstairs. Ziggy's mom, who was already in the kitchen cutting onions for dinner, smiled at them and said, "It be a fine morning for young doodles like you two. Make sure you eat something before you leave."

Ziggy grabbed two onions, took a big bite of one, and said with his mouth full, "We'll be playin' basketball, Mum. Be back soon."

Rico, who usually had cereal and juice and toast in the morning, just like the picture on the front of the cereal box, was always surprised at what Ziggy ate for breakfast. Yesterday Ziggy had eaten a cold ear of corn covered with peanut butter. "Don't be afraid to try new ideas," Ziggy had said. "When we're spies for the FB of I, we may have to eat bugs!" Rico hoped not, but he didn't tell Ziggy.

They were both laughing as they left Ziggy's house and headed for the basketball court down the street. They practiced bouncing their basketballs on the sidewalk at exactly the same time, so that only one *thunk* could be heard instead of two.

Laughing and concentrating, they didn't even hear Jerome sneak up behind them. He knocked both balls out of their hands, yelling, "And Washington's famous come-from-behind sneak attack takes the ball from the two rookies once again!"

"You think you so slick, Jerome-mon," said Ziggy. "But I knew you were there all along. I just wanted you to think I didn't see you."

"Yeah, I forgot, Ziggy, that you were in training—"

"To be a spy for the FB of I," Rico and Jerome shouted in unison.

Jerome lived with his grandmother and two little sisters. Some days he couldn't come out to play with the other guys because he had to babysit. Once, he took his sisters with him to the basketball court, and LaTonya had fallen and bumped her head on a rock. She had screamed like her head was split wide open, even though it was just a tiny bloody spot. She couldn't wait to tell Granny, of course, and after Granny had given her a little plastic bag of ice to put on it, she got great pleasure in announcing to Jerome, "Granny said you can't ever take us down there anymore. You gotta stay here with us until she gets back!"

So Jerome felt good today. School was out, LaTonya and Temika had gone shopping with Granny, and he had the morning free to shoot a few hoops with his friends. Rashawn had called earlier, hoping he would be able to play today.

Rashawn lived at the very end of the street with his mother and his dad, who was a police officer. He had a dog, a Siberian husky named Afrika with one blue eye and one brown eye and a large white stripe down his nose. Everybody said Afrika was crazy. That dog had once chewed a hole right through the wood of Rashawn's garage—just because he didn't feel like being locked up that day. Ziggy said Afrika was the best watchdog in the neighborhood because all he ever did was watch people. He never barked; he just stared at people who came to the house. No one ever knew if he was going to attack or go back to sleep.

When Rico, Ziggy, and Jerome got to Rashawn's house, they yelled, "Hey, Rashawn! Come on out." Afrika just yawned. Rashawn, wearing army boots and dark sunglasses, came out of his house, not with a basketball, but with a large, black plastic dinosaur.

"What's up with the dinosaur?" asked Rico. "That's awesome!"

"A brontosaurus!" yelled Ziggy. "My favorite, mon!"

"It's an apatosaurus, not a brontosaurus," Rashawn corrected him. "They were vegetarians, just like me."

"I still don't believe you don't eat hamburgers or hot dogs or pork chops, man," Jerome chimed in. "I just couldn't make it if I had to live on lettuce and bean sprouts, like you."

"If an apatosaurus could get this big and strong

just eating vegetables, then I guess I'll be okay," Rashawn replied, smiling. "Let's go shoot some hoops and I'll show you who's got the power!"

Rashawn—tall and skinny; Jerome—short, strong and tough; Ziggy—who jumped and bounced and was never still; and Rico—the only one with his shirt neatly tucked inside his shorts, raced one another to the end of the street, where the city had put up two basketball nets for the neighborhood kids. The older, high school kids usually didn't come out until later, so Rico and his friends had the courts to themselves this time of day. Rashawn, the fastest runner, got there first, even though he was holding the dinosaur. Then he just stopped and looked around in disbelief.

"What's up with this?" he exclaimed.

"Why would anyone want to do something so awful?" moaned Ziggy softly.

Rico and Jerome were speechless. Someone had taken a chain saw and cut the basketball poles into little pieces.

TWO

"So what are we s'posed to do now?" Jerome asked angrily. The four friends were sitting on Jerome's front porch, their basketballs tossed uselessly in a corner.

"We could see if we could go to Morgan Park to play ball," suggested Rico, but without much hope in his voice.

"Fat chance, mon," said Ziggy. "You know your mum won't let you go to Morgan Park. It's ten blocks away and on the other side of the freeway."

"Yeah, Rico," Rashawn teased. "Your mama still pins notes on your shirt to take to the teacher!"

"That's not true!" Rico protested. "My mama's just . . . careful, that's all. Besides, at least I got a shirt, Rashawn!"

"O-o-owee! He got you, boy!" yelled Jerome. Ziggy was laughing so hard he was about to fall off the porch.

Rashawn, who was not about to be capped by Rico or Jerome, smiled and replied, "Yeah, but all your mamas wear army boots, and none of them are going to let us go to Morgan Park!"

At that, all of them, even Ziggy, got quiet. They were stuck for the entire summer with nothing to do. The neighborhood swimming pool had been closed because kids kept jumping the fence at night and last summer a boy had drowned. The baseball field had been covered over to make a larger parking lot for the shopping center and there were no movie theaters or video arcades within walking distance. All they had was that small park with the basketball courts, and now it was useless.

"How long do you think it will take them to fix it?" asked Jerome.

"By the time you have a *son* in the fifth grade," said Rico, sighing.

Rashawn, who was still holding the huge plastic dinosaur, said, "Maybe when my dad gets back from his club meeting he can take us to the movies or something."

"Hey, that be sounding real good, mon," said Ziggy. "What kind of club meeting does a grown man go to, anyhow?"

"It's called the Black Heritage Club and they sponsor African American activities and raise money for worthy causes."

"Worthy causes like basketball courts?" asked Rico.

"No, worthy causes more like helping kids to go to African American colleges," replied Rashawn. "But I know the cops will try to find out who trashed our court."

"Well, that's cool too," said Jerome. "But until then we're still stuck right where we were before."

"Maybe not, mon," said Ziggy with a grin. "Why don't we start our *own* club? We could have secret meetings and code words and handshakes and plan spy trips, just like the FB of I!"

"Hey, Ziggy! That's an awesome idea!" said Jerome. "We could have meetings right here on my front porch. That way if I have to watch LaTonya and Temika—"

"No way, man," said Rashawn. "We don't want any little sisters finding out our secret stuff."

"He's right," Rico added. "We need to find a clubhouse or someplace where we can make our plans and hide our treasures."

"Treasures?" Ziggy's eyes lit up. "Of course, we gotta have treasures! We'll bring whatever we can find from home, and then, if that's not enough, we'll go on a mission to search for more!"

"What are we gonna call our club?" asked Rico. "We need a name that's really tight."

"How about Junior Spies of the FB of I?" suggested Ziggy.

"No, man," said Jerome patiently, "none of that FBI stuff. How about the Basketball Posse?"

"That's dumb," said Rico. "Besides, we won't be

playing basketball. Let's call it the Black Stallions. I saw a really good movie about a cool black horse."

"Yeah, like we all got black horses to ride," said Rashawn, who was swinging the plastic dinosaur by its neck. "I know—why don't we call our club the Black Dinosaurs?"

"I like it, mon!"

"Me too," agreed Rico, "and Rashawn's dinosaur can be our mascot."

"We can hang it from the door of our clubhouse!" said Jerome.

"What clubhouse?" Rashawn looked around.

"The one we're gonna build!" Ziggy answered eagerly. He jumped from the top step of the porch. "Let's go! I know the perfect place!"

Three

The four boys ran up the street to Ziggy's house, tossing the dinosaur between them as they went. They headed for the backyard, which was almost like a real jungle. The grass was never cut. It was a place where flowers, weeds, rabbits, and ten-year-old boys could grow wild. An old rope swing still hung from a tree, even though the tree had died years ago. A path, probably used by raccoons, ran back into the thick underbrush. At the very end of this path was what was left of an old wooden fence. Ziggy explained to his friends that the fence had once been a property divider, but now was just fallen lengths of wood. It must have been about six feet high and a hundred feet long when it was first built. Now it was sitting in the sun, waiting to be a clubhouse for the Black Dinosaurs.

"So, what do you think?" asked Ziggy. "No one can see us from the house. It's a perfect place to plan spy missions!"

"It's hot," complained Jerome. "And I hate bugs and thorns!"

"So, as soon as it's built, we'll put in air-conditioning, okay?" said Rashawn.

Jerome grinned. "You make sure you do, and while you're at it, put in a swimming pool too."

"Sure, Jerome," said Rico, smiling, as he sat on one of the fence boards. Ziggy's backyard always amazed him. Rico's tiny little backyard, with its neat rows of pansies and petunias, was nothing like this wonderful jungle. It was a place to dream and to create—a perfect place for a secret clubhouse.

Rico looked at his friends. "We're gonna have to plan this out carefully. We need to borrow tools from home, and we have to remember to bring ice water or punch whenever we're working. There's plenty of wood here, and it won't be hard to put these large sections together to make a clubhouse. It can even have a door and a window."

"I knew it!" shouted Ziggy. "The Black Dinosaurs are now in business!"

They spent the next few days cutting the weeds and bushes to make a clearing big enough for the clubhouse. Jerome's grandmother gave them rakes and garden shears, and Ziggy's mom kept a jug of Jamaican iced tea on the back steps. They finally talked Rashawn's father into letting them use his tools, and after many reminders from Rico's mom about being careful and avoiding snakes, the clubhouse began to take shape.

For the back wall they used a part of the fence that was still standing and sturdy. Connecting the other parts to it was a little shaky at first, but somehow Rico seemed to know what would hold and what angle would work. They cut holes that looked a lot like windows in the two side walls, and for the door, they used a smaller section of the fence that fit perfectly into another hole that Rico cut. They closed it with a bent piece of wire coat hanger.

Rashawn looked a little worried. "How are we gonna put a roof on it?"

"Never fear. I have a plan!" Rico replied with a smile.

Lifting the roof was the hardest part, because the piece of fence they used was very heavy, plus it had been covered with little brown bugs that scrambled everywhere when they lifted it up. Jerome had threatened to quit right then, but Rico ran home and got a can of bug spray, and they were able to get the roof on, with the help of two stepladders, a two-by-four balanced on a rock, and quite a bit of luck.

The clubhouse was finished on Friday morning. Rico and Rashawn grinned at each other with satisfaction. Ziggy bounced with excitement, going in and out of the windows and opening and closing the front door over and over again. Jerome sat on the dirt floor, a cold glass of iced tea in one hand

and a can of bug spray in the other, quietly nodding his head in approval.

The clubhouse was about ten feet by twelve feet—not really big—but large enough for four boys to sit and talk.

Ziggy, looking around with satisfaction, announced, "Let's bring the chairs in."

"I found a lawn chair that my dad was gonna throw out," offered Rashawn. "It's a little bent, but it'll do."

Rico dragged in a chair that had been left behind at a church picnic, and Jerome had found a three-legged kitchen chair. "We can use a rock to balance it," he suggested.

Ziggy grinned as he brought in an old bicycle with two flat tires. "The kickstand still works, mon."

This was their seating arrangement, or they could push everything aside and sit on the blanket that Ziggy's mom had left on the back steps. She never asked questions and never asked to see what they were doing, but she always seemed to know exactly what they needed.

Hanging from the ceiling by a string around its neck—they couldn't figure out any other way to do it—was Rashawn's dinosaur.

Jerome stared at the dinosaur. "Really mellow."

"Awesome," said Rashawn. "You oughta be an architect, Rico. It turned out just like you said it would. How'd you know that?"

"I don't know." Rico shrugged his shoulders. "I just feel it and most of the time it works."

"We gotta have our first meeting and make up rules," said Ziggy. "Okay, the first meeting of the Black Dinosaurs is officially called to order. Rule one: Everyone who comes into the clubhouse must first touch Rashawn's dinosaur—for good luck."

"Good idea," agreed Jerome, "but he needs a name."

"His name," Rashawn proclaimed, rising from his seat in the three-legged chair, "is Blackasaurus!"

"Blackasaurus it shall be!" Ziggy proclaimed, with a bow to Rashawn. "Now for the secret password."

"It should change every day," suggested Jerome.

"No, just every week," said Rico, "'cause we won't meet every single day."

"Okay, mon," agreed Ziggy. "What's the password for this week?"

"How about 'Tuskegee'?" said Rashawn.

"That's a good one," agreed Rico. "Don't forget it now. No one will be admitted into the clubhouse without the password."

"Accepted," said Ziggy. He was really enjoying his role as monitor of the meeting.

"Should we have officers like a president and a treasurer?" asked Jerome.

"No, let's just take turns. Whoever is sitting on the bike is president for that meeting," suggested Rico.

"Sounds good to me!" said Ziggy, who was sitting on the bike. "Now, what about a secret handshake?"

"That's stupid," said Jerome. "We don't need that."

"Okay," said Ziggy. "We do need treasures, though. At the next meeting, we will each bring one official treasure to be donated to the Black Dinosaurs."

Jerome looked at his watch and said, "We better hurry up and adjourn this meeting. I gotta baby-sit."

"Agreed," said Ziggy. "We'll meet again tomorrow at noon with the treasures, mon!"

Four

It was just before noon the next day, and Jerome was the first to arrive at the clubhouse. He didn't want anyone to see the treasure that he had hidden under his shirt, and he wanted to spray for bugs before the others got there. Satisfied that all the bugs were outside the clubhouse, instead of inside with him, Jerome touched the dinosaur for luck, then sat down on the bicycle. "I think I'll be president for today," he said to himself.

A knock sounded at the door. "What's the password?" shouted Jerome.

"Tuskegee!" cried Rashawn. Jerome opened the

door and Rashawn entered, carrying a large brown paper bag. Rashawn touched the dinosaur and said, "What's up, Blackasaurus? What's up, Jerome? Where's everybody else?"

Just then Rico knocked and yelled, "Tuskegee!" When Rashawn opened the door, Rico gave Blackasaurus a good swat and sat down on the lawn chair. "Ziggy's not here yet?" he asked.

"No, but can't you hear him?" asked Rashawn, laughing. Ziggy was singing a Jamaican folk song at the top of his lungs, crashing through the uncleared bushes of his backyard.

"He's got a long way to go before he qualifies as a spy for the FBI," joked Jerome.

Ziggy knocked on the door and yelled, "Open up, mon. Ziggy has arrived!"

Rico stuck his head out the window and said, "What's the password, Ziggy?"

Ziggy smacked himself on the forehead and groaned. "I forgot!" he yelled. "But you know who I am. You just called me Ziggy!"

"Rules say you gotta say the password," said

Jerome, who had stuck his head out the other window.

"Tyrannosaurus!"

"Nope."

"Tapioca!"

"You might be out there all day!"

"Tahiti!"

"You're getting closer—sorta."

"I know it. Wait a minute . . . it's coming to me . . . it's a college—a famous black college . . . uh . . . it's . . . Morehouse. No . . . wait—I remember. I remember. It's . . . TUSKEGEE!" The door swung open and Ziggy barreled through the door.

"Maybe a password isn't such a good idea," he said. "It could hurt a mon's brain, to have to think so hard on a Saturday."

"No way, man," said Jerome. "We gotta make a harder one for next week, just to watch you try to remember it!"

"Did everyone bring a treasure?" asked Rico.

"For sure, mon," said Ziggy. "Just wait till you see what I brought!"

"I've got one too," said Rashawn.

"Me too," said Rico.

"And I do too, so let's begin," said Jerome. "Since I'm president for today, I'll go first." He reached under his T-shirt and pulled out a small item wrapped in a paper towel. Silence filled the club-house as Jerome unwrapped the object.

When the last layer of paper toweling had been removed, Rico asked quietly, "What is it?" It was a small, carved wooden box with little metal bars nailed to the top.

"This," Jerome answered, "is a kalimba. It's an instrument that's played in Africa. My grandmother made it when she was a little girl, and she told me *her* grandmother had showed her how to make it."

"What does it sound like?" asked Rashawn.

Jerome carefully plucked the metal bars. The music was strange and mysterious, but somehow familiar to the boys. "I bet it has magical powers, mon," Ziggy whispered.

Rico said, "My treasure isn't magic, but it's got power. I got it in Chicago when I went to visit my

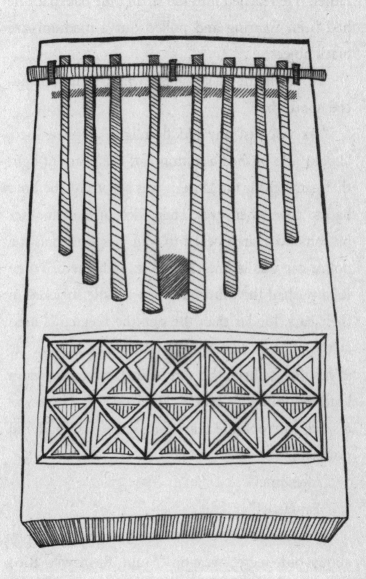

father." He reached into the small blue backpack he had been wearing and pulled out a medium-size black object.

"A flashlight?" asked Rashawn. "What's so special about that?"

"It's not just any old flashlight," replied Rico. "Look!" He pushed a button and the beam of light that came from the lantern was so bright the boys had to cover their eyes. Then Rico pushed another button and a siren began to wail. It sounded as if a police car was in the clubhouse with them. When Rico pushed the third button, a whistle shrieked in their ears, louder than the one the lifeguards used at the pool. Finally he pushed the last button. He said softly, "Check this out." What came out was a loud, booming, **"CHECK THIS OUT!"** There was a small microphone that made any voice loud and powerful.

"Awesome!"

"Fantastic!"

"Turn it off! We don't want anyone to know about our secret weapon!" said Rashawn. Rico turned their secret weapon off and grinned with delight.

Jerome asked, "What's your treasure, Rashawn?"

Rashawn reached into the paper bag and removed a large metal box. It was a little dented, but it was sturdy.

"A box?" asked Rico.

"A safe!" replied Rashawn. "My dad said we could have it. It has a combination lock that really works. We can keep our treasures in it and no one will ever find them."

"What a good idea!" said Jerome. "Will they all fit? Wait a minute. Ziggy, what's your treasure?"

Ziggy had been twitching impatiently and looked as if he were about to explode. "Wait till you see, mon! Just you wait!" He reached into his pocket and slowly removed a package wrapped in tin foil. "Is the door locked?" he asked. "This is super-secret-spy-stuff."

"Yeah, man," replied Jerome. "As locked as it's gonna get. What's that you got there?"

Ziggy slowly unwrapped the foil.

"Oh, boy!"

"Wow, again!"

"Do you think we'll get in trouble?"

"You worry too much, Rico-mon," said Ziggy. "What possible harm could these be?" Ziggy held out a large package of firecrackers.

Five

"Firecrackers!" shouted Rashawn. "Awesome!"

"Those will be our last-chance secret weapons," said Jerome. "We won't use them unless we absolutely have to. We better keep them in the safe for sure!"

"My mom would kill me if she found out we had firecrackers," Rico said nervously.

"That's why the meetings of the Black Dinosaurs have to be kept a secret," Jerome replied. "We're not going to do anything stupid with the firecrackers. It's just nice to know we have them if we need them."

"I know," said Rico, " but my mom is always bugging me about being careful."

"Your mum has raised you well, Rico-mon," said Ziggy. "But not to worry. These are called pop-bangers. Any kid in Jamaica can buy them at the corner store. All they do is make noise. Wanna see?"

"No," said Rashawn. "Let's not waste them. We'll save them for a special Black Dinosaur celebration."

"Agreed," said Jerome. "Let's put the treasures in the safe. Rashawn, what's the combination?"

"Five-ten-fifteen," said Rashawn.

"That's easy to remember. Even Ziggy can remember that!" Rico said, laughing.

Jerome placed the treasures carefully into the safe and locked it. "Now what? Where should we keep the safe? Anybody can come in here and take it."

"You're right," said Rashawn. "These things are too special to just leave sitting in here."

"So what would a good spy do with his secret weapons?" asked Ziggy. "Bury them, of course!"

"Of course!" yelled Rico. "We've gotta bury our treasures!"

Jerome stood up. "I'll go get a shovel."

"I'll go borrow my dad's shovel," said Rashawn, "but I gotta take it back before he gets home."

"I can get a shovel too!" said Ziggy. "There's one in our garage."

Jerome and Rashawn returned in a few minutes with large, sturdy digging shovels. Rashawn's dog, Afrika, followed behind him.

"Why'd you bring him?" asked Rico.

"He can be our watchdog," replied Rashawn.

"Yeah, right. He can watch as spies and robbers take our secrets and treasures. He might even show the robbers where we hid our stuff," said Rico with a chuckle. Afrika ignored Rico and flopped down in the shade.

Ziggy showed up a few minutes later, also carrying a shovel, yelling, "Tuskegee—I remembered!"

Rashawn grinned at his friend. "You only need the password at the beginning of the meeting, but we're proud of you for remembering."

"What's that you've got, Ziggy?" asked Rico.

"A shovel! What does it look like, mon?" Ziggy replied.

"It looks like a *snow* shovel, that's what it looks like!" Jerome told him with a laugh. "What kinda hole you gonna dig with a snow shovel?"

"You never know when it might snow, mon! You think Ziggy would just grab any old shovel from a dark garage? You saying that Ziggy is scared of the dark and didn't check to see what kind of shovel he got? It's for carrying dirt *away* from the hole, my friend!"

"Okay, man, anything you say," said Jerome. "But now we have only two shovels to dig with."

"So let's take turns. Two people dig for ten minutes, while the other two supervise. Ziggy, you and Rico go first," suggested Jerome.

"Be glad to, mon," said Ziggy. "What looks like a good spot?"

"Back here in this soft dirt behind the clubhouse," said Rico. "It shouldn't take too long."

The boys took turns digging, and before they knew it, the hole was more than a foot deep.

"Just a little bit deeper," said Rico. "We want it to be completely buried."

"My hands hurt," complained Jerome. "It's deep enough."

"Okay, Rico," said Rashawn. "I'm tired too, but I'm gonna take my last turn. Besides, all the Jamaican iced tea is gone. It's about time to adjourn this meeting of the Black Dinosaurs."

Rashawn and Ziggy worked for a few minutes, making the hole deep enough and wide enough to hide their treasure box securely. Even Ziggy was getting tired, when suddenly, his shovel went *clunk!*

"Hey, mon! What we got here? A rock?" asked Ziggy.

Rashawn's shovel had also hit something hard. "No, Ziggy, it's not a rock. I think . . . I mean it looks like it might be . . . Brush that dirt out of the way. . . . I think it's a box!"

"A pirate's treasure chest!" exclaimed Ziggy. "We're rich!"

"Let's get it out!" Jerome cried excitedly.

The boys dug furiously for a few minutes. They even used Ziggy's snow shovel. Slowly the dirt disappeared from around the box, which was about three feet long, one foot wide, and one foot high. It was made of a very thick metal that had once been painted red and was badly rusted.

"It looks awfully heavy. Do you think we can lift it out?" asked Jerome.

"Why don't we just try to open it instead," suggested Rashawn.

"Then we can get the gold out and be rich!" added Ziggy. He wasn't tired anymore. This was what Ziggy called a *real* adventure.

"It looks more like a tool box than a treasure chest to me," said Rico. "Don't spend your gold yet."

Rashawn inspected the box. "The lock looks pretty rusted. I bet a good-size rock would bust it. Let's go for it."

Ziggy found a big rock in the backyard and the lock fell off easily after only a few strong blows. The boys wanted that lock off much more than the lock wanted to stay on.

"Let's open it, mon," whispered Ziggy. He was twitching again. This was just too much to sit still for.

Afrika had been watching the boys with very

little interest. But when they approached the box to open it, he growled.

"What's the matter with Afrika?" asked Rico.

"I don't know," replied Rashawn. "He's never done that before. Just ignore him."

When Rashawn touched the box, Afrika jumped up and began to bark as if someone were stealing his food dish.

"Do you think he's scared?" asked Jerome.

"I think he's nuts!" said Rico. "Hurry up and open it!"

Afrika continued to growl.

"Now I *gotta* know what's in that box," said Rashawn. "I'll hold Afrika. Rico, open the box."

"Me? I'm not gonna open it! Maybe it's not pirate's treasure. Maybe it's pirate's blood instead," said Rico with a frown.

"In the first place," said Jerome, "there probably isn't any pirate treasure buried in Ohio. And blood would have dried up by now."

"So *you* open it."

"I'm not gonna open it. *You* open it!"

Ziggy couldn't wait any longer. He was much too excited to be scared. As Afrika growled fiercely, Ziggy lifted the lid of the box. The boys crept closer to get a look inside.

"What is it?" asked Rico, who still expected buckets of blood.

"Bones!" whispered Ziggy. "It's full of bones!"

Six

"Bones? What kind of bones?" asked Jerome.

"Don't ask me, mon," said Ziggy softly. "I've never seen real bones before."

"Maybe they're dinosaur bones," suggested Rashawn. "If they are, we could really get rich. I heard about some kids right here in Ohio who found some dinosaur bones behind their house, and a museum wanted to give them a million dollars to dig up their backyard."

"So what happened, mon?" asked Ziggy.

"Their parents wouldn't let the museum dig—but the kids got their pictures in the paper."

"Be for real," said Rico. "These couldn't possibly be dinosaur bones. In the first place, they're much too small. And who would put dinosaur bones in a box, anyway?"

"Do you think they're human bones?" asked Jerome fearfully.

"I'm not sure," said Rico. "They don't look like the skeleton in Mr. Kelly's science classroom, that's for sure!"

"What are we gonna do?" asked Rashawn.

Ziggy, who had gotten unusually quiet, finally spoke up. "Hey, guys, we got us a real live mystery—or a real dead one. . . ." He tried to make them smile, but they were too nervous to laugh at Ziggy this time. "We gotta keep this secret and be like spies to find out some answers."

"Shouldn't we tell our parents?" asked Rico. "Maybe there's some kind of dead bone disease floating around in that box."

"We're not gonna touch anything, mon," said Ziggy. "We're gonna close up the box and search for clues. Agreed?"

"Agreed," said Jerome, but he looked scared. "What about you, Rashawn?"

Afrika was still growling and wouldn't go near the box of bones. Rashawn looked at the others and said, "This is really scary, but it's the most awesome thing ever to happen to us! Let's see what we can find out about this mystery. If we can't solve it, we'll tell my dad. He's a cop, you know. Ziggy, you're the spy expert. What should we do?"

Ziggy liked the idea that they were finally taking his spy skills seriously. "First," he said, "we close up the box and cover it over with dirt again—not a lot—just enough so that no one can see it. Then we bury our treasure box like we planned. Then we start looking for clues."

"How?" asked Rico. "We don't even know what to look for."

"We start by asking questions," said Ziggy. "Ask at home and around the neighborhood. Nobody knows what we found, so we're safe to ask anybody. Be cool, dudes. A good spy never lets anybody know what he's up to."

"Let's meet tomorrow at the same time," said Jerome. "The Black Dinosaurs spy patrol is now on duty."

"What if we don't find out anything?" asked Rashawn.

"We will, mon. We will," said Ziggy. "You'll be surprised."

They covered both boxes with dirt and left for home, each a little scared and a little excited.

When he got home, Rashawn carefully put his father's shovel back in the garage and went into the kitchen to wash his hands. He grabbed an apple from the sink and joined his father, who was typing on the computer in the dining room. Rashawn's dad was in charge of the newsletter for the members of their mosque.

"Hi, Dad. You busy?"

"Just finishing up here, Son. What's on your mind? You look a little funny. Are you coming down with something?"

"No, Dad," Rashawn said quickly. "It's just kinda hot. Me and the guys got this new club. You oughta

see the clubhouse we built—it's awesome."

"I'll have to check it out. Sounds like fun, especially since your basketball court got destroyed. As a matter of fact, I wrote an article about neighborhood crime for the newsletter. And all of us at the police department think we might have some clues about who did it."

"Clues?" asked Rashawn.

"Sure. That's the first step in good police work. Investigate all your clues."

Rashawn thought, *I can't believe it! Ziggy was right!* Then he asked his father, "So what have you found, Dad?"

"Well, we're pretty sure it wasn't high school boys, because they liked the basketball courts and used them. But we do think it was someone from the neighborhood."

"How come?"

"The officer in charge of the case told me that they found the chain saw—it had been rented from the store around the corner."

"Who rented it?"

"Old Bill Greene—but he used it to cut down that dead tree in his yard. He said the saw had been stolen from his backyard the day after he rented it."

"Do you believe him?"

"So far we have no reason to think he was the one who cut the basketball poles down."

"Did the police find any more clues, Dad?"

"Well—they found a note."

"A note? Like a message?" asked Rashawn.

"Yes, sort of—it was really strange. It said, 'Them bones gonna rise again.'"

At the word "bones" Rashawn almost choked on his apple. "What do you think it means, Dad? And what do bones have to do with basketball?"

"I don't know, Son. Sometimes police work means checking every detail. If we find out anything, I'll let you know."

"Thanks, Dad." Rashawn wondered if this had anything to do with the bones they had found. He could hardly wait for the next meeting. *I wonder what the other guys have found out,* he thought.

Seven

Jerome sat on his porch and watched his sisters as they quietly took turns braiding each other's hair. He didn't really mind watching them today, because he had a lot to think about. Where did those bones come from? What should they do with them? Would they get in trouble for not telling what they found? And how was he going to find any clues? *Maybe Granny will know something,* he thought. *She's lived in this neighborhood all her life.*

Just then Temika and LaTonya started to argue. "It's my turn to play with the black Barbie!"

"Nuh-uh! You had her yesterday. Jerome! She won't let me see the black Barbie!"

Jerome couldn't understand why Granny didn't just buy two of everything and save him the trouble of listening to them argue. But he told them, "Temika, why don't you get the crayons out and color all the Barbies in the coloring book any color you want. LaTonya, you play with black Barbie for a while, then let Temika see her, okay?" The girls seemed satisfied for the moment, and Jerome was glad to see Granny getting off the bus at the corner.

"Granny, wanna see the picture I colored?" Temika yelled from the porch.

"That's real pretty, baby," said Granny as she climbed the steps and sat down on the porch swing. "Jerome, bring Granny a glass of ice water, please. Temika, LaTonya, it's nap time. Go on in there and lie down for a few minutes."

"But Granny, we're not even sleepy," protested Temika, who was six and thought she was too old to have to take a nap.

"You don't have to sleep, child. Just lie down for five minutes with your eyes closed, okay?"

After the girls went inside, still mumbling about not being sleepy, Jerome said, "You know, Granny, one day they won't fall for that trick and they'll stay awake, and we'll have to listen to them all afternoon."

Granny chuckled. "I know, child. You're a good boy to help me with them like you do. You're growing up, and I'm real proud of you."

Jerome smiled. Granny didn't toss out compliments very often. "Can I ask you something, Granny?"

"Sure, child."

"You've lived around here a long time, haven't you?"

"Now, you know that. I was born in that house where your friend Ziggy lives now. Then when I married your grandpa, we moved over here. Your mama was born here in this house, and so were you."

"Did you ever hear about any mysteries when you were little, Granny?"

"The old people always told spooky stories about ghosts and things like that, but I don't remember any mysteries . . . except for—well, that was different."

"What, Granny? Tell me."

"It's nothing really, and it probably isn't even true."

"Tell me, please."

"Well, when I was a little girl, living in your friend Ziggy's house, there was that tall fence all around the backyard—the one you made your clubhouse out of. It was much taller than we were, and it had only one gate, which was always locked, so we didn't have to think about what was on the other side."

When Granny mentioned the fence, Jerome shivered a little. Maybe he was going to get a clue after all.

"Did you ever find out?"

"Yes, but sometimes not knowing the truth is better."

"What do you mean, Granny?"

"On the other side of the fence was a . . . grave-yard!" Granny whispered.

"But, Granny," said Jerome, trying to hide the shakiness in his voice, "there's an apartment building and a parking lot there now."

"Yes, child. They built that more than fifty years ago, when I was just about the age you are now. Some folks tried to complain, but the builders just ignored them and put that apartment complex right over that graveyard."

"Do you think there's ghosts over there, Granny?" asked Jerome. Suddenly the warm summer air felt chilly.

"I don't know. But I do know that when I was about ten or eleven, I used to hear the old folks whisper stuff about boxes of bones. It scared me, so I never asked any questions."

"Granny, what did they—"

"That's enough of that, now. You make me feel cloudy on a sunny day. I don't want to talk about that stuff anymore."

She went into the house to check on the girls, and Jerome sat on the porch, shivering. What had they found? He couldn't sit there alone any longer, so he yelled through the screen door to Granny that he was going over to Rico's house.

Jerome thought Rico's mom acted like the mother on that old TV show, *Leave It to Beaver*. She never had her hair in curlers, never had a dirty kitchen, and never ate pizza. But even though she was what Ziggy called a neat freak, she was always willing to drive the four friends wherever they needed to go. She and Rico were just pulling out of the driveway when he got there.

"Hello, Jerome. Rico asked me to take him to the library. All of a sudden he has an interest in bones—dinosaur bones, he says. Do you want to come along?"

"Yes, ma'am," replied Jerome as he hopped into the backseat. He knew what Rico was up to.

"Any clues?" whispered Rico to Jerome.

"You won't believe it!" Jerome whispered back. "Just wait till I tell you."

Rico's mother dropped them off at the library and told them she'd be back in about an hour. Rico went straight to the information desk.

"Do you have any books on bones?"

"Bones?" said the tired-looking librarian over her glasses. "What kind of bones?"

"Oh, dinosaur bones, chicken bones, pork chop bones, and . . . human bones," said Rico with a nervous grin.

"Try the science section—over there to your left—third shelf down."

Rico and Jerome hurried over and found exactly what they needed—three books on human, animal, and dinosaur bone structure. They put the dinosaur book on top of the pile and walked quickly to the checkout desk, bumping into the old man in front of them in the line, and making him drop his large stack of books.

"You kids watch where you're going!" he said with a growl. "This is a library, not a zoo!"

"Sorry, Mr. Greene," said Jerome, as they helped him pick up his books. "We didn't see you."

"Well, the last time I checked in the mirror I wasn't invisible!" Mr. Greene snapped at them. "But I may as well be for all anybody cares," he mumbled to himself.

Rico and Jerome didn't know what else to say, so they apologized again, checked out their books, and waited in front of the library for Rico's mom to pick them up.

"Did you see the books that Mr. Greene was checking out?" asked Jerome.

"Yeah—kinda weird—they were all on cemeteries and stuff. Here comes my mom. Let's get out of here."

As Rico's mom drove them back home, they sat in the back seat, turning the pages of one of the books they had checked out, looking at the pictures, then quietly looking at each other. They were scared. The book in their hands was called *Bones of the Human Body*.

Eight

They were almost home. Rico's mom turned the corner to their street and then slowed the car. "What in the world is *that*?" she asked in amazement. There seemed to be a two-headed man walking down the sidewalk.

Rico and Jerome looked out and burst into laughter. "That's Ziggy, Mom!" said Rico. Ziggy was walking on his hands, with his feet straight up in the air. On each foot he had placed a baseball cap, so that from a distance, he looked like a man with two heads walking down the street.

"Can you let us out here, Mom?" asked Rico.

"We need to talk to Ziggy. Besides, maybe we can turn him around!" She laughed, shook her head at Ziggy's silliness, and told Rico to be home by suppertime.

"Hey, Ziggy! What's up?" asked Jerome.

"Not me, mon. How do you like my disguise?"

"It's great if we ever need a two-headed man," Rico replied with a grin.

Ziggy giggled, lost his balance, and tumbled into a cheerful heap on the grass, knocking Rico down as he fell. Jerome jumped in, and the three of them tussled and wrestled, until they heard Afrika barking as Rashawn crossed the street and headed toward them.

"What's happenin', dudes?"

"Not much now, mon, but I got clues to report," said Ziggy. "Just wait till you hear!"

"Me too," said Rashawn and Rico in unison.

"And my Granny told me some stuff that will fry your brain," said Jerome.

"I think we need an emergency meeting of the Black Dinosaurs," said Rashawn. "I'll race you!"

The four of them ran down the street, Afrika barking and darting among them, almost knocking them down. Ziggy started yelling simply because he liked the sound of his own voice and because he was in front. The others followed closely behind.

Ziggy got to the clubhouse first, touched the door, and said, "The password is 'Tuskegee'! I remembered!"

"We gotta change the password," Rico told the others. "It's no fun if Ziggy can remember it." Each boy touched the black dinosaur that was hanging above their heads and found a seat.

"Well, men," began Rashawn. "Let's get started. Let me tell you what I discovered!"

He told them about the police investigation and the strange message that said, "Them bones are gonna rise again," and how old Mr. Greene had rented the chain saw that destroyed their basketball court.

"Mr. Greene?" asked Rico in amazement. "We saw him at the library. He was checking out books on graveyards!"

Jerome gasped. Then he told them about the covered-up graveyard and the stories of boxes of bones that had frightened even his grandmother.

Rico opened the library book on human bones. The pictures confirmed that what they had found was probably one of the rumored boxes of bones. It was so quiet in the clubhouse that the boys could hear their own breathing.

Ziggy finally broke the silence. "Very good spy work, gentlemen! But wait till you hear what the greatest spy that ever worked for the FB of I has discovered, mon!" He took a deep breath and began.

"Last night, about midnight, I couldn't sleep so I got up to get a drink of water. I looked out the back window and I thought I saw something. It looked like someone or something was out there by our clubhouse, so I decided to check it out."

"In the middle of the night?"

"By yourself?"

"In the dark?"

"Would you have still gone if you had known about the graveyard?" asked Jerome.

"No way, mon. Ziggy is brave, but he's not stupid. Anyway, the moonlight was bright, so I tiptoed out. No one saw me. No one heard me. I was slick!"

"So what did you find? A rabbit? A squirrel?" Rico asked, his eyes wide.

"No, mon. I saw Old Mr. Greene with a flashlight and a stick, walking where the fence used to be, singing to himself. When he saw our clubhouse, he stopped and stared at it for a long time, but he didn't touch it. Finally he cut through to his yard and went home."

"Do you think he's got something to do with the box of bones?" asked Rashawn. "And since he was the one who rented the chain saw, maybe there's a connection to what happened to our basketball court."

"Could be, mon, because you know what he was saying, over and over again?" asked Ziggy with mystery in his voice.

"What? Tell us!" they all begged him.

Ziggy loved being dramatic. He sang in a soft, scary voice:

"I KNOW IT, KNOW IT,
INDEED I KNOW IT, BROTHER,
I KNOW IT, YEAH—
THEM BONES GONNA RISE AGAIN!"

Rico covered his mouth with his hands. Jerome's eyes opened wide, and Rashawn just about fell off his chair. Ziggy couldn't help laughing, even though he, too, was really scared.

"So what do we do now?" asked Jerome.

"We gotta see what Mr. Greene is up to," replied Rico.

"So how we gonna do that? Stay up all night?" asked Rashawn.

"That's it, mon!" shouted Ziggy. "Let's sleep out tonight, right here in the clubhouse! We'll tell our parents that we want to have a campout, which is true. They don't have to know that we're in the middle of solving a case."

"Let's do it!" said Rico eagerly. "Everybody bring food, a flashlight, and a sleeping bag. Be back here at nine o'clock—it will be just about dark."

"What about bugs?" asked Jerome. "Don't more of them come out at night?"

"So bring bug spray," replied Rashawn. "I'm more scared of ghosts than bugs." At the mention of ghosts, they all looked at one another, but no one backed out.

"Tonight at dark," said Rico softly, "the password will be . . . 'Nairobi.'"

Nine

Rico got to the clubhouse first that night.
He was glad, because his mother had given him
so much stuff he was afraid the others would laugh
at him. In addition to his sleeping bag and a huge
bag of food, she had made him take a rope, a first-aid
kit, hiking boots, and a raincoat. It had been useless
to argue with her, so he just dumped the stuff in
a corner as soon as he got there. The clubhouse
seemed different at night. Outside, the sounds of
crickets and birds seemed louder. The light was fad-
ing fast, and the shadows looked funny on the clubhouse walls.

Rico was relieved when Rashawn showed up, shouting, "Nairobi, dude!" He was carrying a baseball bat.

"What's that for?" asked Rico.

"Ghosts," replied Rashawn. "You just never know."

Jerome knocked just then. "What's the pass-word?" asked Rico.

"Nairobi! Hurry up and open the door before I drop this stuff." He brought in a box of Twinkies, a six-pack of soda, and a bag of potato chips.

"Junk foods—my favorite vegetables, mon," said Ziggy from the doorway of the clubhouse.

He was about to enter when Rico yelled, "What's the password, Ziggy?"

"Oh, no, not again!" moaned Ziggy.

"Oh, yes—you gotta say the word. Now what is it?" Jerome asked him with glee.

"Let's see—Norway!"

"Nope!"

"Nashville!"

"Not even close!"

"Nigeria!"

"You almost got it!"

"I know it—I know it! It's . . . Nairobi!"

They all cheered and laughed as Ziggy bowed and walked in, carrying an extra-large pizza his mom had ordered for them. "No sweat, mon, no sweat. I got a mind like a steel trap." He reached up to give the dinosaur a good whack for luck. "Hey! Where's Blackasaurus? He's gone, mon!"

"What?" said Rashawn, suddenly angry. "I hadn't even noticed."

"Me neither," said Jerome. "Someone's been in here. Why would they take our dinosaur?"

"Our treasures!" said Rico suddenly. The four boys ran outside and began to scrape away the loose dirt and leaves that hid their treasures and the mysterious box of bones. Neither had been touched. They breathed a sigh of relief and brought the treasures inside the clubhouse. Rashawn unlocked their treasure box and made sure everything was still there. It was just about dark.

"Anybody scared?" asked Rico.

"Not yet," said Rashawn, "but I think I'm gonna be. Let's eat."

They spread out their sleeping bags on the dirt floor, placed their flashlights in a circle, like a campfire, and sat cross-legged, gobbling pizza and guzzling pop. Rashawn carefully removed the pepperoni and gave it to Ziggy, who cheerfully ate it up.

"So what do we do if Mr. Greene comes?" asked Jerome.

"Do you think he took Blackasaurus?" asked Rashawn.

"Why would a grown man want a huge plastic dinosaur?" asked Rico.

"Lots of questions—not many answers, mon," said Ziggy mysteriously. "First we wait—then we watch. Answers will appear . . . you'll see."

It was quiet in the clubhouse. Jerome walked around, checking each corner with his flashlight for bugs. Ziggy made shadow animals on the walls, and Rashawn practiced making Boy Scout knots in Rico's rope. Rico sat on the sleeping bags, knees up to his

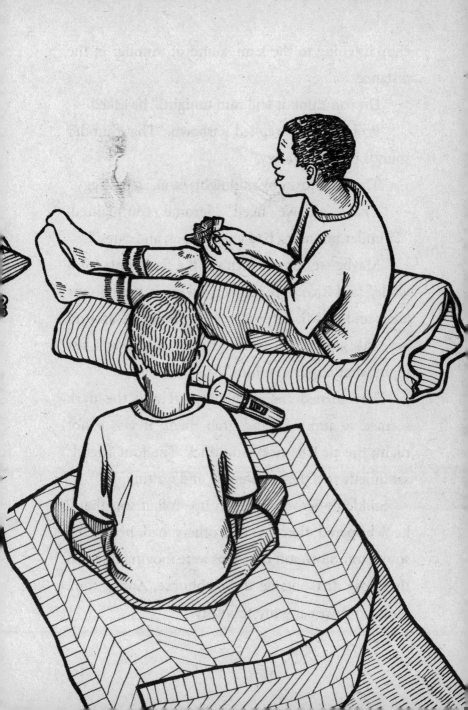

chin, listening to the faint sound of thunder in the distance.

"Do you think it will rain tonight?" he asked.

"Probably not," replied Rashawn. "That thunder sounds pretty far away."

"Thunderstorm by midnight, mon," said Ziggy.

"That's all we need," Jerome complained. "Thunder boomers, bad guys, bones, and bugs!"

"Maybe we should turn off the flashlights for a while," said Rico. "We might need the battery power later, and if Mr. Greene comes snooping around here, it's got to be quiet and dark, like it was last night when Ziggy saw him."

They turned the flashlights off and the dark seemed to jump in and grab them. It was a hot night; the air felt sticky and thick. The four friends sat quietly together—listening and waiting.

Suddenly Jerome jumped up. "What was that?" he whispered fiercely. The others had heard the sound too. Slow, soft footsteps were moving through the loose dirt outside the clubhouse. And a thin, scratchy voice sang mysteriously:

"I KNOW IT, KNOW IT,
INDEED I KNOW IT, BROTHER,
I KNOW IT, YEAH—
THEM BONES GONNA RISE AGAIN!"

"It's him!" whispered Rico. "What should we do?"

Ziggy put his hand over Rico's mouth to stop him from speaking again. "Just wait," he said softly.

As the old man continued to sing, the boys could hear the sound of dirt being shoveled. He dug for a few minutes in one spot, then moved a few feet down and started to dig again.

The boys held their breath. Mr. Greene was digging at the exact spot where the box of bones was hidden. Soon they heard a *clunk* as his shovel hit the box.

"I found it!" he yelled to the sky. "The past cannot be buried! I will destroy the destroyers!"

Then Ziggy sneezed.

Instantly Mr. Greene was silent and turned his attention to the clubhouse. "Who's there?" he growled. He raised his shovel like a weapon and beat on the clubhouse door. "You rotten kids—come outta there! I'll bury you! I'll bury you!"

At the word "bury" Rashawn screamed and jumped out of one window; Jerome jumped out of the other. Mr. Greene pushed open the clubhouse door, held his shovel in front of him like a weapon, and walked directly toward Rico, who was huddling in the corner. Mr. Greene had to crouch a little because of the low ceiling, but that only made him look scarier. In the moonlight, his face was wild and angry.

Just as it looked like he was about to strike Rico, a loud, booming voice behind him roared, "PUT DOWN THAT SHOVEL, MON!"

Startled, Mr. Greene spun around to face a blindingly bright light. He put his hand up to shield his eyes, and a police whistle blew directly in his ears. The siren of a police car pierced the air so close that it seemed to be right there in the clubhouse. Suddenly the rat-a-tat-tat of what sounded like bullets rattled at his feet. He ran out the door, hands up, yelling, "Don't shoot—I didn't do anything!" Outside, there was only darkness.

He took one more step before falling forward into a pile of leaves, tangled in the rope that Jerome and Rashawn had strung outside.

"We got him, mon!" cheered Ziggy, who once again shone the flashlight into Mr. Greene's face.

"So now what do we do?" asked Rico, holding the baseball bat.

Just then an earsplitting crash of thunder rocked the night.

Ten

The flash of lightning that followed the thunder brightened the whole scene for just an instant—four frightened boys surrounding an angry old man tangled in a rope on the ground. Rico held the baseball bat, Ziggy held Rico's treasure flashlight, Rashawn held the empty pizza box like a shield, and Jerome had his finger on the trigger of the can of bug spray—ready to fire.

"I'll get you kids for this!" Mr. Greene screamed at them. "I'll destroy you all—all the destroyers!" Then, just as the next booming clap of thunder exploded around them, Mr. Greene bowed his

head and burst into tears. The boys lowered their weapons and looked at one another in confusion.

"I've never seen a grown man cry before," said Rico uncomfortably.

The wind suddenly started to blow harder and the first large drops of rain splashed the scene. Mr. Greene, who no longer looked so scary, sat weeping on the ground in front of the clubhouse, not noticing the rain, not even noticing the boys.

"Let's take him inside, mon," said Ziggy. "We're gonna get a big storm real quick."

Not knowing what else to do, they helped Mr. Greene up and led him into the clubhouse. They set him gently on the lawn chair. Rico gave him a Kleenex and Rashawn offered him a grape soda. No one knew what to say, so for a moment they just listened to the thunder and the storm and wished they were home in their own beds.

Then Ziggy screamed. Everyone jumped up. Jerome made a dash for the door, even though it was pouring rain.

"What's wrong?" shouted Rico. "Don't scream like that!"

"We're leaking, mon! There's water dripping on my back! It spooked me for a second, that's all."

"Don't do that kinda stuff, man," said Jerome. "We got enough to deal with tonight."

"So what are we gonna do about the leak in the roof?" asked Rashawn.

For the first time Mr. Greene spoke up. He had wiped his tears and was breathing normally. "Why don't you take that raincoat over there and put it on the roof where it's leaking? Put a rock over the coat to hold it down. That's what we used to do in our tree house when we were kids."

They just stared at him for a minute, amazed that this scary old man used to be a kid. Then Ziggy grabbed the raincoat, dashed out into the rain, and covered the leak. A minute later, he ran back in, soaking wet, but smiling again.

"Many thanks, mon," said Ziggy. "So, you gonna tell us what's wrong?"

"Or should I get my dad, who's a cop!" said

Rashawn with a hint of a threat in his voice.

"It sounded like you had the entire police department right here in your clubhouse," said Mr. Greene, chuckling. "What I wouldn't have given to have a wonderful toy like that when I was your age."

"Why did you try to hurt us?" asked Rico, who still held on to the baseball bat.

"And what were you digging for?" asked Jerome. He figured there was no way Mr. Greene could know that they'd found the box of bones.

"And where's Blackasaurus—my dinosaur?" Rashawn asked angrily.

"I'm sorry I frightened you boys. I just wanted to scare you away. I wasn't going to hurt you."

The thunder continued to rumble, and the lightning flashed, while the rain beat steadily down on the roof of the clubhouse. Ziggy wrapped a blanket around himself, and the four boys huddled in the center of the cabin, away from the windows, which let in a very wet breeze. Mr. Greene sat in the middle, relaxed, as if he were glad to finally have someone to talk to.

"Hey, mon," said Ziggy with a smile, "you gonna tell us the real deal?"

"I'll do better than that," replied Mr. Greene. "How about if I tell you a story?"

"That'd be cool," said Jerome. "But no scary stuff—it's not that I'm scared—but Rico here, he can't deal with it."

"Not me!" Rico protested. "Rashawn is the one who jumps out of his skin every time the lightning flashes!"

"Aw, man, quit that," said Rashawn. "All of us were ready to split a minute ago."

"Okay, now," said Ziggy. "Let the mon tell his tale!"

Eleven

"My grandfather, whose name was Mac," began Mr. Greene, "came to Ohio in 1860. He was a runaway slave. I don't know how much you boys know about the old days, but back then, black people in the South were slaves. Boys your age would work from sunup to sundown in the cotton fields. They never got to build clubhouses or play basketball or even go to school like you do."

"We learned about it in school," said Rico, "but I never really talked to anybody who knew about slavery for real."

"Talk to the old people," said Mr. Greene. "They

know more than you think. It's just, no one asks them."

"My grandmother knows a lot of that stuff," said Jerome. "She even gave me a kalimba that her grandmother taught her how to make."

"Treasure it," continued Mr. Greene. "The memories are special. Don't destroy the past."

"What does that mean, Mr. Greene?" asked Rashawn. "You kept screaming about destroyers and stuff—before you started . . . uh . . . crying."

"I'm not ashamed of my tears, son," said Mr. Greene. "Let me finish my story, and I'll tell you what everything means, okay?"

"Okay."

"Anyway, Ohio was what they called a Free State, meaning that slavery wasn't legal here, so when my grandfather crossed the Ohio River, he was free, unless the slave catchers found him and caught him and took him back."

"I read about that stuff in my history book, mon." Ziggy frowned. He looked at Mr. Greene. "That was so not fair!"

"I hear you, son. But slaves were worth a lot of money." Mr. Greene was silent for a moment.

"Did your grandfather get caught?" Rico asked.

"No, he didn't," Mr. Greene replied, continuing his story. "He got a job on the river, right here in Cincinnati, got married, and named his first son Victory. Victory grew up and married my mama."

"So what does all this have to do with you digging in the middle of the night behind our clubhouse?" asked Rashawn.

"I'm gettin' to that part, son. I was the last child born to Victory and my mama—in 1925—so that makes me more than eighty years old."

"Wow!" said Ziggy. "You're old, mon!"

Mr. Greene smiled. "My granddaddy was eighty years old when I was born. He used to tell me stories about slavery and the big house and running away and working on the docks of the Ohio River. He also used to sing the old songs to me. My favorite was, 'Them Bones Gonna Rise Again.'"

Rico gasped. Ziggy wiggled. The thunder was

getting weaker, but the boys hadn't even noticed.

Then Rashawn said, "My dad said that there was a note with that message left near the chopped-up basketball poles."

"That was no message. I dropped it. I'm trying to write down all the old songs that my grandpa taught me. See, here's the rest of the pile." He took from his pocket dozens of slips of paper with titles and words to songs. "I'll finish this someday."

"Powerful stuff, mon," said Ziggy.

"Anyway, my grandpa Mac," Mr. Greene continued, "lived to be ninety years old. I was just about your age when he died. I was heartbroken, because he was my best friend. They buried him in the old cemetery behind this fence.

"Then, just a couple of years later, a company called Burke Builders came in with legal papers and building equipment and covered over the cemetery and put up the apartment building. My parents and some of the other people in the neighborhood tried to stop it, but no one would listen. Nobody really cared about a cemetery filled with poor black folks."

"So is that your grandfather in the box we found, mon?" asked Ziggy, hiding his face in his hands.

"Shut up, Ziggy!" said Jerome. "He didn't even know we had found the box!"

"Oops!"

"So you found the box? I'm glad you did. You probably made it easier for me to locate it tonight. And no, that's not my grandfather in the box—I don't think."

"What do you mean?" asked Rashawn.

"The building company covered over the burial sites, but some bones got unearthed and were tossed aside like trash. My father and I gathered them and put them into the metal box that you found and buried it next to the fence. So what you found in that box is the spirit of thousands of freed slaves and escaped slaves and hardworking black men and women who weren't allowed to rest in peace. It's nothing to be scared of."

"That's a righteous tale, mon," said Ziggy solemnly.

"But we still don't know who cut down our basketball poles," said Jerome.

"I do," said Mr. Greene softly.

"Who is it?" asked Rashawn. "I'll get my dog to get him!"

"I've seen your dog," said Mr. Greene. "He wouldn't bite a mashed potato."

Ziggy burst out laughing. "He's got you there, mon!"

"Who did it, Mr. Greene?" asked Jerome.

Mr. Greene sighed. "Seems old Mr. Burke—the owner of the company that destroyed our grave-yard—has a son who runs it now. The son wants the land where your basketball courts are, to build an apartment building there. He figured if the neigh-borhood thinks the park is dangerous and likely to be vandalized, he would be able to buy the land cheaply."

"No way, mon!" said Ziggy, jumping up. "We won't let him!"

"And how are we gonna stop him?" asked Rico. "Firecrackers?"

"No, with *these!*" replied Mr. Greene with a twinkle in his eye. He pulled three wrinkled photographs out of his pocket.

The boys passed the pictures around with silent wonder, smiling as they realized what they showed.

"How did you manage to take pictures of men with 'Burke Builders' on the backs of their shirts and chain saws in their hands?" asked Rico. "And using those chain saws to cut up our basketball poles?"

"It was easy," replied Mr. Greene. "I wander around the neighborhood a lot. Nobody pays any attention to me because everybody thinks I'm just a crazy old man."

"Well, we sure are glad that we found out different, mon," declared Ziggy. "What are you going to do with the pictures?"

"Well, I wasn't going to do anything, because I didn't think it would help," Mr. Greene told them, "but since I've met you boys, I decided that I'm going to turn them over to the police and work to make things right."

"And we'll help you," said Rashawn. "Tomorrow

I'll tell my dad all about this, and I know he'll take care of it. He's a cop, you know."

"I got it! I got it, mon!" screamed Ziggy, knocking over a chair in his enthusiasm.

"Got what? The password? Kinda late, isn't it?" Rico said with a chuckle.

"No, mon—I got an idea!"

"So tell us before you pop!" Jerome said.

"Rashawn's dad is a member of the Black Heritage Club, right, mon?"

"Right. So?"

"I'm sure if they hear about Mr. Greene's grandfather, they'll help to find a special place of honor for that box to be buried, mon."

"Since we found the box, we can get our pictures in the paper and everything!" added Rico.

"We'll be famous!" cried Rashawn.

"And we'll be helping some folks who helped us a long time ago," Jerome reminded them.

Mr. Greene smiled at them all. "That's all I ever wanted, son—I guess I just went about it the wrong way. You know, I bet your dad's Black Heritage Club could also help with rebuilding your basketball court. Have you ever asked?"

"No—we just figured they wouldn't care," said Jerome.

"That was exactly my mistake," replied Mr. Greene. "Don't give up like I did. Go and ask for the help you need."

"You're pretty cool for an old dude, mon," said Ziggy. "We'll try it!"

"Well," said Mr. Greene, "it seems that the storm is over, so I'd better get back home. You boys have a campout to finish. Good night."

He left, whistling "Them Bones Gonna Rise Again." It was quiet for a moment. Suddenly the boys heard a terrible crashing through the underbrush.

"It *couldn't* be a ghost," said Ziggy, who had put his head under the blanket, "could it?"

"No," said Rashawn, laughing. "It's just Afrika, coming to join us. And look what he has in his mouth!"

Slightly chewed, but still in one piece, was Blackasaurus. Afrika dropped the dinosaur at their

feet, wagging his tail to be petted and praised. The boys laughed with relief, and moved their sleeping bags so that the dog had a nice warm spot in the middle of the clubhouse.

The thunder had stopped, the lightning no longer flashed, fear had disappeared like the raindrops, and the Black Dinosaurs curled into their sleeping bags for a good night's sleep.

STUDY GUIDE FOR
Ziggy and the Black Dinosaurs:
The Buried Bones Mystery
by Sharon M. Draper

CHAPTER 1

1. Rico is looking forward to his summer vacation. Talk about vacations and tell what activities you like to do. Discuss the good parts as well as the bad parts about being out of school.

2. Write or draw a description of Rico, Ziggy, Jerome, and Rashawn. What makes each boy unique?

3. How are the families of each of the four boys alike? How are they different?

4. Compare your family to your best friend's family. (Consider foods, family structure, and rules.)

5. Explain why Ziggy is in the bathtub. Have you ever been afraid of the dark?

6. Discuss what Ziggy has for breakfast. Is it healthy? What is the weirdest thing you have ever eaten for breakfast?

7. What career goal does Ziggy have? What do you think he needs to learn about that job?

8. Why do the boys have to play basketball in the morning?

9. What immediate problem faces the four boys?

10. What advice would you give them to help resolve this problem?

CHAPTER 2

1-2-3. Write down three insults the boys make to each other.

4. How do those statements show friendship?

5. How do Ziggy, Rashawn, Rico, and Jerome decide to solve their problem?

6. How do they decide on the name of the club?

7. Discuss any clubs or organizations you have been a member of. What kinds of activities did you do?

8. Have you ever formed your own club? Why would that be fun? What would you call it? What kinds of activities would you include?

9. Why do you think people join clubs?

10. Whose idea is it to build a clubhouse?

CHAPTER 3

1. Describe Ziggy's backyard. Draw a picture of it.
2. What do they use to build the clubhouse?
3. How hard do you think it would be to really build a clubhouse like they did? Explain your answer.
4. Describe the process the boys use to build the clubhouse. Make a list of everything they do.
5. How long do you think it takes to build it?
6. Draw a picture of what you think the inside of the clubhouse looks like.
7. Which boy doesn't like insects? How do the other boys look out for him?
8. Why do the boys decide on passwords and rules? Why are rules like that important for clubs?
9. What is the first password they choose and why?
10. List some of their rules for their club.

CHAPTER 4

1. Describe the treasure that Jerome brings.
2. Why is it important to him?
3. Describe the treasure that Rico brings. Tell all the things it can do.

4. Why is it a good thing to have in the clubhouse?
5. Describe the treasure that Rashawn brings.
6. Why is it a good idea?
7. Describe the treasure that Ziggy brings.
8. What is potentially dangerous about Ziggy's treasure?
9. If you had to bring a treasure, what would you bring and why?
10. What is humorous about Ziggy's inability to remember the password?

CHAPTER 5
1. Rico worries about his parents finding out about the firecrackers. When is it not a good idea to keep a secret from parents?
2. How would you keep the club treasures safe?
3. Why do the boys decide to bury the treasures?
4. Why does Ziggy bring a snow shovel?
5. Do you think the boys actually plan to find anything when they are digging? If you dug a hole in your backyard, what do you think you would find?
6. Describe the box they find.

7. Why do the boys think the box holds treasure?

8. Which boy always seems to offer a sensible solution to every problem?

9. Why do you think Afrika growls as they begin to open the box?

10. Make a prediction. Where do you think the bones came from?

CHAPTER 6

1. Why is it impossible for the bones they find to be dinosaur bones?

2. What information do they need to solve the mystery of the buried bones?

3. What is Ziggy's plan?

4. What do they do with the two boxes?

5. What does Rashawn's father tell him about clues?

6. What does the note say is found near the chopped-down basketball poles?

7. What do you think the message might mean?

8. Why does that note make Rashawn extra curious and interested?

9. Make a prediction. Who do you think destroyed the basketball court?

10. What clues do they have so far?

CHAPTER 7

1. Jerome realizes his grandmother might be an important resource for information. Explain how she could possibly know about what happened in the neighborhood long ago.
2. What information can your parents and your grandparents give you about your neighborhood or your family history?
4. What information does Jerome's grandmother share about their neighborhood?
5. What does she say the old folks used to whisper about?
6. What used to be on the other side of the fence they use to build the clubhouse?
7. Find out if it is illegal where you live to build an apartment building over a graveyard.
8. What information do the boys seek at the library?
9. What kind of books is Mr. Greene checking out from the library?
10. List all the clues the boys have collected so far.

CHAPTER 8

1. Describe the "two-headed man" that Rico's mom sees.
2. Who is it really and what is he doing?
3. What do the boys learn from the book about bones they get from the library?
4. Make a prediction. What connection do you think Mr. Greene has to the destroyed basketball poles?
5. Make a prediction. What connection do you think Mr. Greene has to the destroyed box of bones?
6. What does Ziggy discover about Mr. Greene? Why is this suspicious?
7. What song does Mr. Greene sing? Why is that mysterious?
8. Why does Rashawn think they need an emergency meeting of the Black Dinosaurs?
9. Why do the boys decide sleep in the clubhouse? Have you ever slept outside at night, for example, at camp?
10. Make a list of the items you would take on a campout in your best friend's backyard.

CHAPTER 9

1. List the things Rico's mother has given him for the campout.
2. What does this tell you about her?
3. What is frightening about sleeping outside in their clubhouse?
4. Why do they bring the treasures inside the clubhouse?
5. What has happened to Blackasaurus? What do the boys think has happened to it?
6. What is scary to the boys as they hear Mr. Greene digging and singing?
7. What do you think Mr. Greene is digging for? Why?
8. What does Ziggy's sneeze trigger?
9. Explain Mr. Greene's statement, "The past cannot be buried! I will destroy the destroyers!"
10. List, in order, exactly what happens to Mr. Greene at the end of the chapter.

CHAPTER 10

1. What does the thunder add to the mood of the story?

2. Draw a picture of the four boys and Mr. Greene at the beginning of chapter ten. What is each boy doing? What is Mr. Greene doing?

3. Why does Mr. Greene cry?

4. How do the boys react to his tears?

5. Have you ever seen an adult cry? How did that make you feel?

6. What makes Ziggy scream? Why does this add excitement to the scene?

7. Mr. Greene makes several comments about when he was a little boy. Write a description of Mr. Greene as a child and the kinds of games he played or toys he played with.

8. Why do you think the boys decide to trust Mr. Greene?

9. How safe do you think the boys are in the clubhouse with Mr. Greene? What might have been dangerous about the situation?

10. How has the boys' impression of Mr. Greene changed since they saw him at the library?

CHAPTER 11

1. Create a timeline of Grandfather Mac's life and Mr. Greene's life as he describes it.

2. What do the boys learn about slavery from Mr. Greene?
3. What do the boys learn about Cincinnati and its importance to slaves?
4. How old is Mr. Greene?
5. How does Mr. Greene help to solve the mystery of the song about the bones?
6. How does Mr. Greene help to solve the mystery of the destroyed basketball poles? What proof does he have?
7. What is Burke Builders and what bad things has it done in the past?
8. What do the boys decide to do with the box of bones? Why?
9. What has really happened to Blackasaurus?
10. What do the boys learn about the importance of remembering the past?

ADDITIONAL ACTIVITIES:

A. INFORMATION TO EXPLORE AND DISCOVER. Use the Internet or an encyclopedia or books to find out more about the following:

1. African American Clubs and Organizations
2. The brontosaurus dinosaur

3. Discovering dinosaur bones

4. The Tuskegee Airmen

5. Tuskegee University

6. Nairobi, Kenya, East Africa

7. Siberian husky dogs

8. African American Burial Grounds

9. Hair braiding

10. Bones of the human body

B. JOBS TO EXPLORE:

1. FBI or CIA agent

3. Private investigator

4. Newspaper reporter

5. Photographer

6. Musician

7. Instrument maker

8. Historian

9. Architect or Builder

10. Archeologist

C. WRITING ACTIVITIES:

1. Using newspaper ads from building supply
   stores, find out what you'd need to build your
   own clubhouse, and how much it would cost.
   Write up a plan for your clubhouse.

2. Owning a pet is a big responsibility. Find out all the things you have to do to care for a dog. Write an essay about dog ownership.

3. Interview someone who has lived in your neighborhood or someone who has been in your school a long time and discuss how it has changed. Write an essay about what you learn.

4. Write a poem or story about being afraid.

5. Write a poem or story about friendship.

6. Write a mystery that includes clues. At the end of your story show how the clues are solved.

7. Using a picture of the human skeleton, write an essay about the bones of the human body.

8. Find out all the words to the folk song "Them Bones Gonna Rise Again." Write an essay that tells the origin of the song.

9. Write a newspaper story about how Ziggy and his friends get Burke Builders punished.

10. Write a newspaper story about what Ziggy and his friends and Rashawn's father finally do with the box of bones.

What's next for Ziggy and the Black Dinosaurs?

Turn the page for a sneak preview of their next adventure, *Lost in the Tunnel of Time*.

One

Like cool, sweet milk on a bowl of crunchy cereal, the Thursday morning breeze splashed the crisp, dry leaves under Rico's feet. He liked this time of year. It would soon be time for warm fires in the fireplace and frosty snow on the sidewalk. His mom had made him wear a jacket to school today, and it felt good. As he crossed the street to the school building, he spotted his friend Ziggy and waved.

Ziggy sat on the front steps of the school, digging wildly in his book bag. He pulled out two broken pencils, a half-eaten apple, a red spiral notebook, a sandwich wrapped in plastic, a doorknob, and a green tennis shoe. "Hey, Rico-mon! Did you do your history homework?"

Rico chuckled. "Sure, Ziggy. It was easy. Didn't you do yours?"

"Of course I did it, mon—Ziggy is no fool. But I can't *find* it!"

Ziggy continued to empty the contents of his book bag on the school steps—his math book, seven small smooth rocks, five nickels, and a purple three-ring binder. "It's gotta be in here somewhere," he mumbled to himself. His long braided hair, covered with a small, green and yellow knitted cap, hung over his shoulders.

"What are the rocks for?" asked Rico.

"I call them the Seven Special Stones of the Sun," replied Ziggy mysteriously as he held the rocks in his hand for Rico to see.

"Why do you call them that? What makes them so special?"

"My grandmother gave them to me, mon. She brought them all the way from Jamaica. She told me they would bring me good luck."

"They look like ordinary rocks to me," Rico said with doubt.

"Well, that just shows how much you know, mon," Ziggy said as he rolled the stones in his palm. He looked thoughtful, then asked, "Can you keep a secret, Rico?"

"Sure," replied Rico, who never knew what Ziggy would do or say.

"These stones . . ." Ziggy paused for a moment. He looked around to make sure no one was listening. His voiced dropped to a whisper. "These stones keep away *ghosts!*"

"Ghosts?" Rico laughed nervously. "There are no ghosts around here!"

"See how well the stones are working, mon?" Ziggy replied with glee. Rico laughed again, shaking his head at his friend. Ziggy plopped the stones back into his book bag.

Just then a gust of wind blew through the schoolyard and across the steps. The pages of Ziggy's red notebook fluttered and gently released the one sheet of paper that had been tucked inside. Ziggy's large, round handwriting boldly filled both sides of the paper.

Ziggy grabbed it triumphantly. "I found it, mon! Let the bells ring and the school day begin!"

The early bell seemed to hear him, for the signal to go into the building sounded just as he spoke. Ziggy stuffed the rest of his things back into his bag, tossed it over his shoulder, and called to Rico, who never ceased to be amazed at Ziggy, "Let's go, mon. We'll be late!"